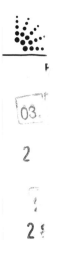

For Isaac and Oliver
A.F.

For Sarah and Jim
P.D.

First published 2007 by Walker Books Ltd
87 Vauxhall Walk, London SE11 5HJ

2 4 6 8 10 9 7 5 3 1

Text © 2007 Anne Fine
Illustrations © 2007 Penny Dale

The right of Anne Fine and Penny Dale to be
identified respectively as author and illustrator of this work
has been asserted by them in accordance with the
Copyright, Designs and Patents Act 1988

This book has been typeset in Giovanni Book

Printed and bound in Great Britain
by Creative Print and Design (Wales), Ebbw Vale

British Library Cataloguing in Publication Data:
a catalogue record for this book
is available from the British Library

ISBN 978-1-4063-0180-9

www.walkerbooks.co.uk

Jamie and Angus Together

Anne Fine
illustrated by
Penny Dale

Other books by Anne Fine include:

Contents

The Very Mysterious Present

Jamie pushed a chair up
to the table to have a serious talk
with Angus, his little Highland bull.
He stood Angus so the two of them
were nose to nose, then looked
deep into his eyes.

"Bella's coming to tea," he warned his favourite soft toy and his very best friend. "Remember Bella?"

Angus looked anxious.
Perhaps, thought Jamie,
he was remembering
the time Bella threw
him up so high he
hit the ceiling.

Or the time
Bella squashed his
stumpy little legs.

Or the time Bella dropped him in the paddling pool, and he'd had to stand on the radiator for nearly a whole week to get dry, and then have the worst of the tangles brushed out of him.

No wonder he wasn't looking too happy.

"It's not *my* fault she's coming," Jamie explained to Angus. "*I* didn't invite her. Mummy did. She's very friendly with Bella's mother, and Bella's just tagging along to save them getting a babysitter."

Angus didn't stop looking doubtful.

"She doesn't *mean* to be rough," Jamie told Angus. "It's just the way she is. Mummy calls her bouncy and Daddy says she doesn't stop and *think*." He scowled. "And *I* think she just sails into other people's houses and treats their toys as if they belonged to *her*."

He pulled Angus closer to cuddle him. "This time," he promised, "I am going to protect you. You wait and see."

9

Angus didn't look
confident and Jamie
could understand why.
Jamie had tried to protect
him from Bella before.
Once, when she came,
Jamie had rolled Angus
up inside his pyjamas
and hidden him in his
bed. But Bella had
suddenly started
her own roly-poly-
over-Jamie's-bed
game, and he'd
had to pull Angus
out fast. Bella had
snatched Angus
and, before Jamie
could stop her,
had thrown him
up at the ceiling
– really hard.

The next time Bella came, Jamie
had carried a stool all the way
along the hall so he could
hide Angus on the top shelf
of the bookcase. But while
Bella was rushing one of
Jamie's teddies to her play
hospital, her sharp eyes had
noticed Angus peeping out
from between the books.
She'd dragged Jamie's toy box
out of his bedroom so
she could stand

on it to fetch Angus down.
Then she had put Angus
in her hospital and
squashed his poor
little stumpy legs
all over the
place while
she looked
at his tummy.

11

The last time Bella came was the worst.

In desperation, Jamie had hidden Angus at the bottom of the garden, deep among the daisies. But when Bella got as high as she could on Jamie's climbing frame, she'd suddenly spotted Angus's little grey horns poking out above the flowers. She'd hurried over to see whose horns they were, then snatched Angus up to cuddle him. Jamie ran to the rescue and crashed into her by mistake.

Bella had let go of Angus and he'd sailed over the lawn and landed – *splosh!* – in the paddling pool.

"She doesn't mean to be horrid," Jamie told Angus again. "She just gets noisy and bouncy. She really can't help it."

But Angus was still looking terribly trembly.

Jamie made up his mind. "This time," he promised his best friend in the whole wide world, "I'm going to hide you somewhere even Bella won't find you."

Where was the best place?

In the fridge, among the lettuces in the plastic drawer at the bottom?

No. Far too cold.

In the oven? But someone might decide to turn it on, and Angus might get cooked by mistake.

No. Definitely not in the oven.

14

He could wrap Angus up carefully and hide him in the rubbish bin. Bella would never look there. But even if he warned his mother, she might get busy and forget. Without even thinking she might put the bag in the wheelie bin. Then the bin men might come along and— Jamie couldn't bear to think about what might happen after that.

Just then, the doorbell rang.

Out of time! While Mummy went to open the door, Jamie grabbed Angus and ran to the nearest cupboard to hide. In it was all the stuff Jamie's mother and father used to send letters and post parcels. There were envelopes and piles of paper. There were boxes and cardboard tubes. There was sticky tape. There was a pile of odd bits of wrapping paper left over from birthdays and Christmas. There was even a box of fancy stick-on ribbon roses.

The cupboard was full to bursting. But Jamie still managed to squeeze in somehow, with Angus trembling in his arms.

And that was the moment when Jamie had his brilliant idea.

From inside the cupboard, Jamie could hear Bella running down the hall, calling out his name. He heard her opening the doors to all the rooms, looking for him, then banging them shut again. She thundered upstairs to see if he was there. Her shouts and thumpings and bangings were so loud they covered all the noise Jamie and Angus were trying so hard not to make in the cupboard. They covered the

sound of the wrapping paper unfolding around Angus's hooves. They covered the sound of the sticky tape unravelling. They even covered the rustling in the box of ribbon roses.

Footsteps came closer. Jamie could hear his mother calling him. "Jamie, you have to be polite. Come out and play with Bella."

Jamie took a deep breath and pushed open the cupboard door, ready to crawl out. "We have to be very brave now," he whispered to Angus. "And we have to wish ourselves luck."

All afternoon, a very mysterious present sat on the table.

"Who is it *for*?" Bella kept asking everyone. "There isn't a label on it and that's really strange."

That wasn't the only strange thing about the present. It was a very peculiar shape and covered in all different sorts of bright shiny wrapping paper. The bits were stuck together with sticky tape, like patchwork.

And there were ribbon roses all over it, as if someone had wrapped the present in the dark, squashed up in a small space, then stuck a rose over every little hole and tear in the paper, and another over every messy crumple.

If you looked carefully, you could see two tiny spyholes at the front, as if someone hidden in there might be peeping out.

And if you looked even more carefully, you'd see, just underneath, two even tinier holes, as if somebody might possibly need them for breathing.

Bella wasn't the looking carefully sort.

All she noticed was the bright glossy paper and the ribbons sparkling all over.

"Perhaps it's for me," she kept telling everybody. "It doesn't say who it's for, so it might be for me."

"I don't think it's for you," Jamie kept telling her back.

"We could open it and see," said Bella.

Did the present
tremble? Jamie thought
it did.

Perhaps Jamie's mother
saw the little tremble too,
because she suddenly
said, "I'm sorry, Bella,
but it's a rule that you
can't open a present
unless it's definitely
for you."

She winked at Jamie.

If Jamie had been able
to do it yet, he would
have winked back.

"Let's go and play little lost bear cubs," he said
to Bella. "You'll like that game. It's rough
and noisy and bouncy and you
don't have to *think*."

After tea, when Bella had
gone safely back to her own house,
Jamie's mother lifted the very mysterious present
off the table and handed it to Jamie.

"I think this might be for you," she said, smiling.

"Yes. I think it might be too," Jamie admitted.

He took his time unwrapping it.
Playing with Bella had been
a lot of fun because she was
really rough and noisy and
bouncy and didn't *think*,
and that was the best way
to play bear cubs.

But unwrapping Angus
would be better. It would be just as
wonderful as unwrapping him when he first came.

No.

It would be even better this time, because he'd
had him long enough to love him even more.

Angry Eggs

Jamie had a big fat colouring book
full of pictures of boats and princesses,
cars and birds, toadstools and houses,
and hundreds of other things. There
was even a little Highland bull that
looked almost like Angus.

Jamie liked setting out all his wax crayons in a row, then choosing which colour to use. Angus would help him. Then Jamie would colour in the picture, trying hard not to go over the edges, while Angus stood and admired him.

Some of the pages in the book were blank.

"Draw me something to colour in," Jamie said to Daddy.

So Daddy drew two huge shirts flapping on a washing line and a mouse sitting on a barrel, and Jamie coloured them in.

Then Jamie went to Mummy. "Draw me something to colour in."

Mummy drew a very angry egg with beetling brows and a fine moustache. Jamie coloured it in.

Then Daddy drew Jamie a sea horse with lots of babies. Jamie chose a different coloured crayon for every baby sea horse, but they were all so small he kept going over the edges.

He went back to Mummy. "Draw me something else, please."

Mummy drew another very angry egg with beetling brows and a fine moustache.

"You already did that," said Jamie.

"I know," said Mummy. "But it's the only thing I can draw."

"Why?" Jamie asked. "Is it easy?"

"Very," said Mummy. And she showed him exactly how to draw an angry egg with beetling brows and a fine moustache.

Jamie drew angry eggs all that day, and most of the next. Sometimes he didn't even bother to colour them in. He just drew the next egg instead. On Thursday, Flora the babysitter picked him up from nursery school.

"What did you do today?" she asked.

"We had the easels out," Jamie told Flora. "And I drew angry eggs."

When they got home, he drew another, just to show her how.

"You're quite the artist!" Flora said admiringly. "And now I know exactly what to make you for your birthday."

On Jamie's birthday, there was a present from Flora so big it had to be left lying flat on the floor.

"Go on, unwrap it," said his father.

Jamie tore off the paper. It was a home-made easel, painted all over with daisies. And as extra surprises on top of their other presents, Mummy and Daddy had cleaned all Jamie's paintbrushes till they looked new again and refilled his paint pots. Uncle Edward had bought him a big plastic apron from the charity shop, and Nana had found him an old hat with a feather sticking out of it.

"Now you can be a proper painter," said Mummy. "You don't have to just do angry eggs. You can paint anything."

Jamie put on the apron and the hat with the
feather. He set out the paints and the brushes, and
filled the water pot.

Now he was ready! He put Angus on the table, so
he could watch, then stood in front of the beautiful

home-made easel Flora had given him
and used his pencil to draw an
angry egg. Then he coloured it in
with the paints, trying not
to splash over the edges.

Nana came round for tea. She looked at Angus
standing patiently on the table. Then she looked at
the angry egg.

"It doesn't look *much* like Angus," Nana said.
"Is it an abstract?"

"What's an abstract?" asked Jamie.

"It's a painting that doesn't look much like the
thing it's supposed to be."

"No," Jamie told her. "It's not an abstract. It's an
angry egg. Angry eggs are the only things I can draw
for myself, so that's what I'm drawing."

"But you're *painting* now," Nana pointed out
to him. "And painting is different from drawing.
You don't need black lines around the edges. If you
look at things properly, you'll see they don't have
black lines around them anyway. That's just for
colouring books."

33

Nana took the brush. "Here," she said. "I'll show you." And she painted Angus standing patiently on the table. She didn't put any black lines around him at all; and when Jamie looked at Angus properly to see if they were missing, he noticed Angus didn't have any black lines around him anyway. He looked more as if he drifted fuzzily into the background.

Nana handed the brush back. "Have a go," she said.

So Jamie tried painting Angus. He dipped his brush in the most Angus-y coloured paint and started with Angus's little tub of a body, and his four sturdy legs. Jamie added a head and a tail. Then he switched to a darker colour and painted in Angus's eyes and hooves.

"The legs look a bit wobbly," he admitted. "And one of the horns is much longer than the other. His eyes are in the wrong places too. Perhaps it's an abstract."

"Perhaps it is," said Nana.

As soon as she'd gone, Jamie drew one more angry egg to cheer himself up, then said to Daddy, "Can I paint your portrait?"

"Certainly," said Daddy.
"Flattered and proud. Give me
a moment to make myself comfy." He fetched
a large gin and tonic and a dish of olives, then
picked up the newspaper and stretched himself
out on the sofa with his feet up.

"I can't even *see* you," Jamie complained. "You're
completely hidden behind the paper."

"Don't worry about that," Jamie's father reassured
him. "It'll just look more like me."

So Jamie dipped his brush into the grey and
painted the newspaper. Then he rinsed and used red
for the sofa. He dotted in what was left of the olives
in green before turning to blue for the carpet.

Just as Jamie finished the portrait, Mummy came home from work. She took a look. There wasn't any of Daddy in the painting at all – just sofa and olives and the newspaper.

"It's an abstract," Jamie explained to her. "Can I do you next?"

"I'm a bit pushed," said Mummy.

"Please!" Jamie said. "I don't mind if you move a little bit. Daddy never moved at all, and it wasn't any easier."

So Mummy perched on one of the stools in the kitchen and waited while Jamie dragged his new easel over to face her. He was about to start painting, when the phone rang and she rushed off to answer it, so he began with the stool.

It was a long call, so he painted the ceiling as well. Finally she came back. He was about to paint her, when she remembered there was something in the freezer she wanted to defrost, and she slid off the stool again.

Until she came back, Jamie painted the fridge instead.

Mummy climbed on her stool again. He was about to paint her, when the washing-machine stuck on spin as usual.

"Can you get that?" she called to Jamie's father.

"I wouldn't want to risk it," Jamie's father called back. "You know you're the only one who's sure exactly where, and exactly how hard, to kick it."

So Mummy slid off the stool again, to kick the washing-machine on from spin.

While she was doing it, Jamie painted the oven on the other side of her stool. What with the ceiling, the oven and the fridge, he had used up a lot of his white paint.

At last she came back.

"Ready," she told him again.

Jamie looked at his painting. By now there was hardly any room left in the picture to put her. He'd painted the oven so wide on one side and the fridge so wide on the other, that he had to squash his mother in between them, paintbrush thin.

She looked more like a *stick* than a person.

"It's an abstract," Jamie told her defensively when she came over to look. And he drew another angry egg to cheer himself up.

Jamie kept painting all week. He painted everyone who came to the house. Flora ended up looking like a wheelbarrow. ("Time I went on a diet," she murmured.)

Uncle Edward looked like a beetle. ("I must try to get out more," he muttered.)

And Mrs O'Hara from down the road looked like a rather strange table lamp. ("He's captured my arthritis to a T!" she said. "Lambkin!")

Jamie still uses his easel. He often puts on his apron and sets out the paints and brushes and his little pot of water. He even puts on his special hat with the feather.

But he mostly paints angry eggs with beetling brows and fine moustaches. He uses a stubby black pencil to do their edges, just like in a colouring book. Then he paints them in while Angus stands and admires him.

Whenever Nana comes, he quickly pins her old portrait of Angus up over whatever he's painting.

Nana winks, and says his painting is getting better and better. Then she draws him a really angry egg – much, much fiercer than any of Mummy's, and with much thicker black lines so Jamie won't even have to try too hard not to go over the edges.

And Jamie's painting *must* be getting better, because he almost never does.

Let's Pretend

Jamie and Angus were in the back room
playing let's pretend. Today they
were horses. Angus was grazing peaceably
on one of the green bits of the carpet,
and Jamie was drinking from the
blue border around the edge.

"It's easier for you," Jamie told Angus. "You've got the right sort of nose for eating and drinking off carpets."

In came Jamie's mother. "Remember you're sleeping at Nana's house tonight? Ready to go?"

"But we're busy being horses," said Jamie.

"You can be horses over there," said Mummy.

"No, we can't," Jamie told her. "Nana's carpet has all the wrong colours for playing horses."

"Then you'll have to think of something else you can be," said his mother.

On the way over to Nana's, Jamie and Angus thought about what else they could pretend to be.

"How about ghosts?" Jamie whispered.

But Angus looked as if he thought playing ghosts might be a little too scary in someone else's house, even a house where he felt as safe as he did at Nana's.

"We could pretend we're builders," suggested Jamie.

But it was obvious from the look on Angus's face that he thought playing builders might be a little too noisy for Nana.

Jamie kept thinking. "I could be a prince, and you could be my trusty steed," he said. Then, just in case Angus wasn't quite sure what a trusty steed was, he added, "That means you'd be my favourite horse, and we'd go everywhere together."

Angus looked happy enough with that.

Then Jamie had another idea. "Or I could be an orphan," he said. Just in case Angus didn't know what an orphan was, he added, "That's someone who's lost their mother and father."

Angus looked very anxious.

"But I'd still have you," said Jamie. "My best and only friend in the whole wide world. And even really sad orphans cheer up in the end."

Angus looked happier.

For the rest of the journey, Jamie tried to choose between the two ideas. Orphan? Or prince? It was so difficult that by the time they turned into Nana's street he still hadn't decided. "I know," he whispered to Angus. "I shall be both. I'll be an orphan prince."

Nana waved Jamie's mother goodbye and turned to Jamie. "How are you?" she said.

"I'm very well, thank you," Jamie replied most

politely. "My name is
James. This is Angus.
And it's so very kind of
you to offer us shelter
from the storm."

"Not at all," Nana
assured him, though
she looked a bit startled.

As they went into
the house, Jamie gave
Nana's silk jacket
a little tug and she
bent down so she could
hear him whisper.

"Now, you mustn't be at all *put off*," Jamie
informed her. "But I shall be *staring* at everything
in your house as if I've never seen it before."

"Really?" said Nana. "Is there any particular
reason?"

"Yes," Jamie said. "Angus and I are playing let's
pretend. And I'm an orphan prince."

"I see," she said. "And what's Angus?"

47

"I'm not quite sure yet," Jamie confessed. "During the orphany bits, he'll be my best and only friend in the whole wide world. But in my more princely moments, he might have to turn into my trusty steed."

"It sounds a bit complicated," said Nana.

"Yes," agreed Jamie. "I think it is, a bit. We were just playing simple old let's pretend we're horses before, but I'm afraid you've got the wrong carpets."

"Sorry about that," said Nana. She threw open the door to her living room. "Welcome, Your Highness, to my humble home."

Jamie tugged her down so he could whisper. "You don't *know* I'm a prince yet. Until I tell you, you just think I'm a sad orphan."

"Even more complicated than I thought," said Nana. She stood up for a moment, then almost at once bent down again to whisper, "One last thing. Would you like me to be cruel, or kind?"

It was another very difficult decision.

"Do *cruel* first," Jamie suggested.

Nana drew herself up. Her eyes flashed and she pointed a witchy finger at Jamie and Angus. "Ha ha *ha*!" she cackled. "Now that you're in my clutches I shall set you to work. Mop all the floors and wash the windows till they sparkle! And be sure not to spill a single drop of water, or that precious Angus of yours will go into my broth pot!"

"Do *kind* now," Jamie told her hastily.

Nana bent down to put an arm round Jamie and pat Angus's snout. "You poor, poor dears!" she told them. "How horribly you must have suffered! But all that's over now. You'll be happy and safe with me. Would you like some hot soup to warm you after your dreadful journey? Or would you prefer spaghetti? The twirly sort I don't yet know you like."

"We'll have spaghetti, please," Jamie answered, ignoring the last bit. And just in case she went back to doing *cruel* again, he added, "And we'll definitely have *kind*, please."

"Fair enough," said Nana, and she sent them to wash their hands and hooves before supper.

Sitting at the table, Jamie began to tell Nana their terrible story.

"It was a happy life," he said. "Angus and I lived in a palace." He lifted his fork and started to twirl his spaghetti.

"Along with your mother and father?" asked Nana.

"Yes," Jamie said. He had to stop twirling to think. "My mother was the queen and my father was the king. And I was the prince." He glanced at Angus in case he was feeling a little left out of things. "And Angus was my best and only friend in the whole wide world and my trusty steed."

"Both at once?" Nana asked.

"Just for now," said Jamie. "Till I'm a bit more sorted."

Before he could twirl up even a single mouthful, Nana was asking him, "So what happened next? How did you get to be a sad, sad orphan knocking on my door?"

"It was dreadful," said Jamie. He hadn't had time to sort this part out yet, so he laid down his fork again to think. Surely there must be something he could use from all the picture books his father and mother read him in bed and on boring afternoons.

He could remember a fairy tale about a frog. A frog wasn't a king, exactly, but Nana was looking at him expectantly across the table, and Angus was waiting.

"My father—" began Jamie.

"The king," Nana reminded herself, twirling another forkful of spaghetti.

"That's right," said Jamie. "Well, my father, the king, dived into a deep pond after a golden ball. And never came out again."

The frog had managed all right, as far as he could remember. But frogs were good with ponds. It was a well-known fact.

"And your poor dear mother?" asked Nana.

Now, just as he was about to take his first mouthful, Jamie had to think some more. This let's pretend was getting as twirly as spaghetti. "My mother, the queen, sat sobbing in a high tower, trying to grow her hair long enough for someone to climb up it to rescue her."

"Fancy that!" said Nana.

Jamie put down his fork again. He knew he was getting in a bit of a tangle but added a few more snippets from stories he half remembered. "And along came the youngest son of a poor farmer. And he could probably have rescued her, but there were three Billy Goats Gruff living under the bridge down the road.

And he forgot to fill his pockets with pebbles that would shine in the moonlight to show him the way. Then a briar hedge grew up and he couldn't get through it because of the spiteful thorns. So he never managed to get to the tower to rescue my mother."

"Shame," said Nana. "A shocking story. Altogether tragic." She lifted another forkful of spaghetti and patted Jamie's hand across the table. "And so you became an orphan?"

"Yes, indeed," said Jamie. By now, his head was twirling almost as much as the spaghetti he still hadn't had a chance to eat. He remembered a bit from yet another story. "And then I had to wander up hill and down dale with a crust of bread wrapped in a spotted

handkerchief on the end of a stick." He saw Angus watching in astonishment. "And kill a dragon," he added, panicking. "And sit among the cinders before spinning a whole load of straw into gold before morning." He could tell just from looking that his supper was practically cold now. Jamie sighed. It had been a whole lot easier playing let's pretend we're horses, grazing peaceably on the green patches of the carpet and drinking from the blue border around the edge.

"What about Angus?" asked Nana, putting the last forkful of her own spaghetti safely into her mouth.

Jamie took a deep breath. He was exhausted and they hadn't even begun on Angus's part of the story.

"He had to try on glass slippers to see if they fitted like a glove,"  he told Nana.

"Then climb up a beanstalk."

"Worse and worse," murmured Nana. "And rather awkward, what with the poor lamb having hooves."

Jamie was on the verge of saying, "Angus is not a lamb. He is a Highland bull." But then he remembered Angus was supposed to be a trusty steed. (And, in the less princely bits, the orphan's best and only friend in the world.)

It was impossible. Impossible. So Jamie gave up. He gave up twirling spaghetti and he gave up twirling stories too. Putting down his fork, Jamie picked up his knife and spoon. First he chopped all his spaghetti into handy little chunks, then he spooned it up fast.

"Angus has had a very hard time too," was all he said.

When Jamie's father came in the morning, Jamie and Angus were packed and ready to go.

"Good time?" asked Daddy.

"It was a little *tiring*," Jamie confessed.

"Never mind," Daddy consoled him. "When we get home, you and Angus can play something quiet until you feel stronger."

So Jamie and Angus did. Together they played let's pretend we're horses. Angus grazed peaceably on the green bits of the carpet while Jamie took the occasional quiet long drink from the blue border that ran around the edge.

A Nice Long Walk in the Country
(Without Any Fussing)

Jamie and Angus were sitting
happily together on the rug, inspecting
their treasure. There were exactly seven
chocolate coins left over from Christmas
– one very big one and six little ones.
Jamie was trying to decide which to eat
next, and Angus was trying to help him.

Should Jamie choose the really big one, just because it was bigger?

Or should he choose one of the smaller ones, just because, afterwards, there'd be more chocolate left?

Suddenly Jamie's mother came into the room holding her coat. "We're all going out for a nice long walk in the country now," she told them.

Uncle Edward looked up from his shiny new magazine all about fast cars and asked his sister, "Why? I'm happy sitting here on the sofa reading, and Jamie and Angus are happy stuffing their faces with chocolate coins."

"Not stuffing our faces," Jamie scolded him. "Choosing between them carefully."

"Sorry!" Uncle Edward corrected himself. "Just choosing between them carefully."

"You'll enjoy it once you're out there," said Jamie's mother.

"I'm already enjoying myself," Jamie explained. "And so is Angus."

"So am I," said Uncle Edward.

"You'll like a nice long walk in the country just as much," insisted Jamie's mother. "It will blow away the cobwebs."

"I don't have cobwebs," Jamie informed her loftily.

"I like my cobwebs," Uncle Edward said. But, sighing, he dropped his glossy new car magazine on the sofa and scrambled to his feet.

Jamie tipped the last seven chocolate coins safely back into their little gold net bag. "You stay here on the rug," he told Angus, "and guard our treasure."

He stood Angus so that his front hooves were one each side of the bag. Angus looked very proud indeed to be left in charge of their last seven

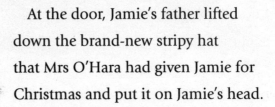

chocolate coins – one very big one and six very much smaller ones.

At the door, Jamie's father lifted down the brand-new stripy hat that Mrs O'Hara had given Jamie for Christmas and put it on Jamie's head.

"Why do I have to wear this?" demanded Jamie. "I'm not even cold."

"Because we're going to walk past Mrs O'Hara's house," said Daddy. "And if you're not wearing the hat she gave you, she'll think you don't like it."

"Well, I don't," grumbled Jamie. "It's hot and itchy."

Jamie's father reached for the matching stripy scarf still hanging from the peg. "All right," he said, wrapping it loosely around Jamie's neck. "You can wear this instead."

"I hate the scarf too," Jamie kept grousing. "It keeps scratching my neck." He scowled. "*And* it makes me look as if a stripy snake is trying to strangle me."

He turned to Mummy, thinking she might stick up for him. But Jamie's mother wasn't even looking at Jamie. She was gazing at one of the photographs on the wall that Uncle Edward had taken the year before Jamie was born. It was

64

a picture of Jamie's mother and father, hand in hand, striding out together across the countryside.

"One day," Mummy said softly and wistfully, "one magic day, maybe we'll get to go for a nice long walk in the country without any fussing."

Uncle Edward gave his sister a long look. Then he reached over and lifted the stripy hat off Jamie's head. "I'll wear this for you," he said.

Then he unfurled the stripy scarf from around Jamie's neck. "And I'll wear this for you too. Then, if Mrs O'Hara looks out of the window, she'll think you were really, really happy wearing the lovely new stripy hat and scarf she gave you, but I liked them even more, and so I borrowed them."

He twisted the scarf around his neck till it made him look as if a stripy snake were trying to strangle him.

"I'm ready now," he announced to everyone. "Bring it on! Rain! Hail! Sleet! Snow! I can face it all."

As they walked past her house, Jamie remembered
to wave at Mrs O'Hara, and she waved back. She
looked a bit sorry for Jamie because he'd had to
lend his brand-new hat and scarf to Uncle Edward.
But Uncle Edward cheered her up by pretending
the stripy scarf was a snake trying to strangle him,
and falling down in the gutter.

At the end of the road, they came to the stile
that led to the walk across the fields. Jamie's father
climbed over first, then held out a hand to Jamie's
mother.

Without waiting, the two of them set off along the footpath across the field.

Jamie climbed over the stile next. He was about to rush off after Mummy and Daddy when Uncle Edward, who was still clambering over, started to grumble.

"Why do they
always decide to put the stile
in the muddiest corner of the field?"

It wasn't often Jamie knew more than a grown-up,
so he couldn't help hanging back to explain.

"You've got it the wrong way round," he told
Uncle Edward. "The reason this corner has got so
muddy is because the stile was here first."

"Really?" said Uncle Edward. He'd climbed over
to the other side now, but he still wasn't walking.
He was looking around as if he'd never been on
a walk in the country in his whole life.

"And why is this field full of giant white maggots?" Uncle Edward asked Jamie. "Those aren't giant white maggots," Jamie told him. "Those are *sheep*." "Sheep?" said Uncle Edward, as if he'd never seen a sheep before. "Well, why are they *staring* at us?"

70

Jamie glanced along the footpath.
Mummy and Daddy were well ahead now,
and they were holding hands. He wished
Uncle Edward would stop fussing, so they could
catch up.

"Those sheep aren't *staring*," Jamie explained
to Uncle Edward. "They're standing looking at us.
Just in case."

"Just in case *what*?" asked Uncle Edward.

"I don't know," Jamie said. "Maybe just in case
we have a big fierce dog with us that rushes over
to attack them."

"They've had plenty of time to see that we don't have a big fierce dog with us," Uncle Edward grumbled. "And they're *still* staring. I believe they *hate* us."

"Of course they don't hate us," Jamie reassured him. "Sheep don't hate people."

"Birds do," said Uncle Edward, setting off along the footpath at last. "Listen. You can already hear them shouting at us to get out of their field."

Jamie was beginning to see what Mummy meant when she talked about having a nice long walk in the country without any fussing. "That's not shouting," he said to Uncle Edward. "That's singing."

"*Singing?*" said Uncle Edward. "You call that *singing?*" He stuck out his chest. "*This* is what I call singing." And he stopped fussing long enough to launch into Jamie's favourite song from nursery school – the one about the bad bunny who went through the forest bopping all the field mice on the head until the good fairy flew down to tick him off and make him be good again.

There were quite a few verses so, what with stopping to argue about the words every now and again, Jamie and Uncle Edward stayed well behind Jamie's mother and father, who were now walking arm in arm very closely together.

Uncle Edward nodded towards them. "See that?" he said to Jamie. "They're clinging to one another because they're frightened the rabbits are going to get them."

"No, they're not," Jamie said. "No one is frightened of rabbits. Nobody in the whole wide world."

"I am," said Uncle Edward. "So I'll stay really close to you." And he unfurled one end of the long stripy scarf and looped it around Jamie's neck so the two of them were tethered together.

It made it rather hard for Jamie to walk without stumbling.

"One day," he scolded Uncle Edward, "one magic day, maybe we'll be able to get through a walk in the country without any fussing."

It didn't seem as if the walk took a particularly long time. But still they went further than usual. From one of the fields they passed, there wafted the most terrible smell from the winter muck-spreading.

Uncle Edward unravelled the end of the long stripy scarf from Jamie's neck, drew himself up to his full height and breathed in deeply.

"Aaah!" he exclaimed. "Lovely! The sweet scent of the countryside! Absolutely enchanting!"

Jamie was pinching his nose closed with his finger and thumb to stop the smell getting inside it. "Yuck!" he kept saying. "Yuck!"

"As gorgeous as *perfume*!" Uncle Edward argued.

Jamie didn't like to say exactly what he thought the muck-spreading smelled like. Instead, he pointed the other way. "Look!" he said.

A herd of cows was watching
the two of them from the other side of a gate.
"Ah, yes," said Uncle Edward. "Antelopes!"
"Cows," Jamie corrected him.

Mummy and Daddy had stopped at the end of
the field. They were hugging each other so closely
that Jamie thought they might even be kissing. After
a bit, they turned and started walking back towards
Uncle Edward and Jamie.

While they were
waiting, Uncle Edward
and Jamie leaned over
the gate to watch the cows.
Suddenly, one of them lifted its tail.
"What *is* that cow doing?"
Uncle Edward asked.
Jamie couldn't help giggling.
Uncle Edward stared. "I can't believe
my *eyes*," he declared. "Jamie, did you see
that? Did you see what that cow *did*? Right in
the middle of the field? With people *watching*?
Did you *see*?"

"No need to fuss about it," Jamie scolded
his uncle. "It happens all the time."

"All the *time*?" Uncle Edward looked horrified.
"That is *disgusting*," he said. He clutched Jamie's arm.
"Careful! Your mother and father are walking behind
us. Don't turn round! We don't want them getting all
upset. Just let them walk on by and get a bit ahead of
us on the way back. Then they won't have to see" –
he shuddered – "anything so *disgusting*."

Jamie's father and mother caught Uncle Edward's last word as they strolled by.

"What's disgusting?" they asked.

"Nothing," said Uncle Edward, still fussing. "I'm not even going to tell you. It's *too* disgusting. Just walk a short distance ahead, please. You'll be much safer."

All the way home, Uncle Edward and Jamie stayed a little way back, and kept their eyes peeled for more disgusting sights that might come as a shock to Jamie's mother and father.

Back at the house, Jamie's mother sank down onto the sofa.

"That was lovely!" she said. "Magic! A nice long walk in the country without any fussing at all." And she patted her brother's hand as he sat down beside her.

Jamie didn't want to tell on Uncle Edward so he said nothing. He just slid the gold net bag out from between

Angus's hooves and tipped the chocolate coins out on the rug to count them.

Angus had done a very good job of guarding them. There were still exactly seven: the very big one and the six little ones. And, this time, Jamie didn't have any problem at all choosing which to eat next. He didn't even need Angus's help.

Jamie picked up the very big coin. It was definitely the one he'd chosen. *Definitely*.

Perhaps Mummy had been right and he'd had cobwebs. And even though Uncle Edward had done an awful lot of fussing all the way to the very last field, and all the way back again, maybe a nice long walk in the country had done the job and blown the whole lot of them away.

Magic!

Something
Different

It was Saturday. Jamie and Angus
were in the bedroom, sharing a few quiet
moments. Jamie was trying to think
of something completely different to do
that day, and Angus was watching him.

Jamie's mother poked her head round the door. "Do you want to come and write the shopping list with me?"

Jamie shook his head. "No, thank you," he said. "Today all I want to do is something completely *different*."

A little while later, Jamie's father put his head round the door. "Want to come and help me make smoked mackerel and potato salad?"

Jamie shook his head. "No, thanks. Today Angus and I want to do something completely different."

"Fair enough," said Daddy. "You'll let us know, I hope, if we can give you a hand?"

"We will," said Jamie. And he sat beside Angus, thinking a little longer.

Suddenly he said, "I know! We'll sort out all the books in my bookcase. We've never done that before, so that's something different."

He turned Angus round, so they could both look at the bookcase. What a mess it was! Some of the books were standing up straight as soldiers. Some were leaning over like long grass in high wind.

Some lay flat. Some were half in and half out. Some
were in messy piles all over the shelf. Some were
squashed, some were loose, and some had fallen
out all over the carpet.

"It's going to be a big job," Jamie warned Angus.
And Angus looked as if he agreed with that.

First, Jamie pulled all the books off all the shelves,
then he went to fetch a damp cloth.

"I'm wiping all the sticky fingerprints off my
bookcase," he informed his father.

When the shelves were clean and dry, Jamie picked up the nearest book. But he wasn't sure where to put it. He could put big books on one shelf and little books on another. But some of the books weren't big *or* little. They were sort of medium.

Or he could put all the red books together and all the yellow books somewhere else. But colours could be difficult. After all, some of the greeny books were a little bit bluey. And some of the bluey books were rather greeny. It was hard to tell.

He wanted to do the job properly, so he went off to get advice.

"How do you *do* it?" he asked Daddy. "How do you sort books properly? Do you put together all the ones you like, and all the ones you don't care about somewhere else? Or do you put the ones you're happy to look at by yourself on one shelf, and the ones you like someone to read to you on another shelf? How do you *do* it?"

Daddy scratched his head. "There are a lot of ways of sorting books," he said. "Sometimes it's by who wrote them. Sometimes it's by what they're about.

Sometimes it's even just by which shelves they fit on. But they're your books, so you can choose any way that suits you."

"Good," Jamie said. "Angus and I will have a think."

Jamie went back and made a space for himself among the heaps on the floor. "We can choose any way of sorting we like," he reported to Angus.

While they were thinking, Jamie wiped a smudge of marmalade off one of the covers. Then he used his fingernails to pick a dried-up smear of cottage cheese off another.

"I could put all the happy books on one shelf and all the sad books on another," he suggested.

Angus looked at *The Bumper Book of Fairy Tales* under his hooves.

"Yes," Jamie agreed. "That one would be a problem. It's really happy in some parts and really sad in others. Where would we put that?"

So they thought some more.

"I could put all the books I like Mummy to read to me up on the top shelf," Jamie said. "And all the books where Daddy does the voices better down at the bottom."

He sighed. "But there are lots of books where it would be hard to choose." He picked up *Goldilocks and the Three Bears*. "I mean, Daddy does the bears' voices much better than Mummy. But he makes Goldilocks sound stupid and I don't like that."

He picked up a joke book. "And I like Nana to read this best," he admitted to Angus, "because she explains the jokes I don't understand, and sometimes she doesn't even understand them herself."

 Jamie picked
up *The Big Book of
Nursery Rhymes* and
opened it at the page
with the huge fat tyre
track across it, from when he'd ridden his scooter
over it in the garden by mistake. "And Flora's best at
singing these," he told Angus. "Because even where
the pages are torn, she still knows all the words.
Will I have to give Flora a shelf of her own?"

It was clear Angus didn't know. And while they
were both worrying, a string of dried black stuff
fell out of *The Big Book of Nursery Rhymes* onto
the carpet.

"That's old lettuce," Jamie confessed to Angus.
"I remember that. It fell in the book when I was
eating a sandwich, and I couldn't say anything
because I was busy chewing, and I couldn't pick it off
because I was using both hands to hold the sandwich.
And Flora didn't even notice it was there because she
knows the words to all the nursery rhymes so well
she wasn't bothering to look. And by the time we

turned the page over, I'd sort of forgotten about it."

He looked at the sea of battered books around him. "I've got a really good memory for books," he bragged. "I can remember which ones have chocolate fingerprints on them, and where I slopped soup when I was ill in bed, and when the jam fell off my toast onto the pages, and where I grabbed them to stop people turning over before I was ready, so the page got torn."

He blushed. "And the ones I scribbled in when I was too young to know better."

To cheer himself up, he said to Angus, "You made a mess of some of them too." He picked up *The Beast in the Bed* and turned to the last page. "See this big splodge where the colour's gone all pale and faded?"

Angus had a look.

"That's you," said Jamie. "That's where you sat on the page almost all day when you were wet once."

He picked up a pop-up book and turned to the page he wanted. "And see this pop-up bit's missing? Well, that's where you got stuck after that bubblegum caught in your tail at the playground. That's why this bit's gone. It tore off with you when I picked you up."

Angus looked suitably embarrassed.

"Never mind," said Jamie. "If you keep reading books, they will get bashed about." He looked at the bookcase. "And it's given me a good idea for something *different*."

Just before teatime, Jamie invited Mummy and Daddy in to see what he'd done.

"My golly!" his mother said. "What a brilliant job! That bookcase is sparkling clean now, and you've cleared everything off the floor."

"I told you I was going to do it properly," said Jamie.

His father looked carefully along the shelves. "How did you choose to sort them in the end?" he asked. "Which way did you decide suited you best?"

Jamie went closer to the bookcase. "These are the

torn ones," he told them, pointing to the top shelf. "And these are the ones with stains in. Here at the bottom are the ones I scribbled in when I was younger. These are the ones with pages missing. These are the ones with fingerprints. And this one here, all by itself, has gone a bit mouldy."

"Well, there you go," said Daddy. "Whatever suits you best. And that is certainly different."

"That's what I told you," Jamie reminded him. "That all I wanted to do today was something *different*."

And off they went to have smoked mackerel and potato salad.

Fun for One

Jamie put Angus on the kitchen table
and looked him firmly in the eye.
"Angus," he told him gravely, "there's
something I have to talk to you about."

 Angus looked rather nervous.

"You mustn't worry," Jamie assured him. "It's just that I've had my birthday now. So I'm a bit older."

Angus looked even more worried.

"Not too old to play with you," Jamie said hastily. "Just too old to play with you *all* the time."

Angus kept listening. But Jamie didn't really feel like explaining any more. He didn't want to tell Angus that sometimes he thought it would be nice to have not just a soft toy to play with, but a real imaginary friend – a friend who could join in all his games properly.

Jamie thought of all the things a real imaginary friend could do but Angus couldn't. It wouldn't be tactful or kind to tell Angus what they were. But Jamie could at least try to get him used to the idea of not always being in every single one of his games.

"From now on," Jamie explained, "I might want to do one or two things without you."

Angus didn't look too happy. But then again, he didn't look too sad either.

On the whole, Jamie thought, the little talk they'd had together had gone rather well.

Next morning, Jamie put Angus on the table again and told his mother, "I'm going to write a book."

He hoped Angus was listening.

"You'll have to write the words for me," Jamie explained. "But I'll do the pictures."

"Righty-ho," said Mummy. She pulled a few sheets of clean paper towards her and stapled them together. Then she twisted the top off her pen. "What's it going to be called?"

"*Fun for One,*" said Jamie.

Jamie's mother took
a quick look at Angus
and then, without saying
a word, wrote very neatly
on the top sheet of paper:

Fun for One
by Jamie

She lifted her head. "OK," she said. "What shall
I write on the first page?"

"'Popping bubble wrap',"
said Jamie. "Angus can't
do popping because
of his hooves."

"He could watch you,"
said Jamie's mother. "And
then you could call the book *Fun for Two* instead."

"No," Jamie said. "Just watching isn't going to
count with this book, because I really want it to be
called *Fun for One*."

"It's your book," said Mummy. "So it's your decision. And now I think about it, I'm pretty sure I have a bit of bubble wrap in my cupboard. Would you like me to look for it?"

"Yes, please," said Jamie.

It was a pretty big sheet that took quite a long time to pop, and soon Jamie was so busy he forgot about the book he was writing until the following morning.

Next day, when Jamie's mother came home from work, she found Jamie waiting for her, holding the pen and paper.

"You have to write in my book for me," he told her proudly. "Uncle Edward came round today and showed me another thing that Angus can't do properly but is fun for one."

Mummy slid off her jacket. "Oh yes? What's that?"

"Holding your breath until you go blue and fall over."

Jamie's mother looked anxious. "I'm not sure that's a very good idea."

"It's not very easy, either," Jamie told her. "I've been trying all day, and I've only gone a bit pink."

"Good!" said his mother. "What about the falling-over bit?"

"I'm nowhere near that," sighed Jamie.

"Show me," said Mummy.

So Jamie showed her. He stood in front of the mirror and took a huge breath. He scrunched his lips tight and puffed out his cheeks like a hamster. Two tiny dots of pink appeared. Then he opened his  mouth and all the breath exploded out again.

"That looks safe enough to me," Mummy admitted, and she picked up the pen.

"Uncle Edward fell over twice," Jamie warned her. "But he was nowhere near blue. He wasn't even *pink*." He scowled bitterly. "I'm pretty sure he was pretending."

"I'm pretty sure he was as well," said Mummy. Then she said, "By the way, if Uncle Edward was with you, didn't that make it fun for two?"

"No," Jamie assured her. "I asked Uncle Edward about that. And he said he wasn't really part of the game at all. He said he was simply there as" – he took another deep breath while he was remembering – "as a temporary safety adviser."

"I see," said Mummy. "And what about Angus?"

"He was only watching," said Jamie. "And I told you yesterday that only watching doesn't count."

Then, because Angus seemed a tiny bit hurt, Jamie tried very hard not to look his way again until he'd drawn two whole pictures: one of himself sitting all alone popping bubble wrap, and the other of him standing by himself on the rug, going blue and getting ready to fall over.

The next day, Jamie climbed into next door's huge old broken pram so he and Angus could enjoy one of their favourite pastimes: watching the world go by. When they got bored, he scrambled down with Angus and went into the house to draw a picture of himself squashed under a big green hooded canopy on the third page of *Fun for One*.

Then he carried it over to Daddy to fill in the words.

"Please can you write 'lying in next door's old pram' for me?"

Daddy looked surprised. "I thought I saw Angus with you in the pram," he said. "Didn't that turn it into fun for two? And shouldn't Angus be in the picture?"

"No," Jamie said firmly. "Because Angus can't twist round by himself, even when something really interesting is happening behind him. He always has to wait for me to turn him."

He checked to see if Angus was looking as hurt as before. But Angus was sitting on the table staring the other way. And that was why lying in next door's old pram had to go in the *Fun for One* book, thought Jamie. Because if Angus couldn't even turn round by himself, it couldn't really be fun for two – not like with a real imaginary friend who could do everything: pop bubble wrap, hold his breath, and turn round whenever he wanted.

All the next morning at nursery, Jamie was thinking about his new imaginary friend. He thought about what he'd look like and what he'd be called. He thought about all the things they'd do together.

As soon as he was back home, he warned his mother: "Today we're going to write down 'have an imaginary friend'. But first I'm going out in the garden to try it, just to make sure it's fun."

He put Angus on the window sill, where he could see out. He looked a bit sad. "You'll be all right here," Jamie comforted him. "I won't be away long. I'm just going to have a little bit of fun for one."

Jamie rushed around the garden with his new imaginary friend, whose name was Boris. First, they had races to the top of the climbing frame. Then they jumped over the flower beds. Then they pretended the paddling pool was full of sharks. Playing with Boris was very different from playing with Angus because Boris could do everything that Jamie could do.

Sometimes a whole lot better.

If Jamie climbed to the top of the climbing frame
as quickly as he could, he couldn't help imagining
Boris climbing even faster.

When they jumped over the flower beds, Jamie
couldn't help imagining Boris jumping even further.

And when they pretended the paddling pool was
full of sharks, Jamie couldn't help imagining that
Boris always saw the biggest ones, and saw them first.

It wasn't much fun.

After a while, Jamie gave up and looked round.
There at the window was Angus, looking as forlorn
and lonely and left out as he had been ever since
Jamie started writing *Fun for One*.

What did it matter, Jamie thought suddenly, if Angus couldn't pop bubble wrap with his soft thick hooves? Or hold his breath? Or turn round by himself in next door's old pram? When Jamie was with Angus, Angus thought every idea Jamie had was a really good one, and they did everything together.

He was still Jamie's best friend in the whole wide world, and they always had good fun, even when Angus was only sitting and watching.

Forgetting Boris, Jamie rushed into the house and lifted Angus off the window sill.

He ran to the table where his mother had left *Fun for One* lying ready for him to draw a picture of his new imaginary friend.

Jamie picked up the book and ran to his mother.

"Can you cross something out for me?" he asked her. "Can you please cross out *Fun for One* and make it say *Fun for Two* instead?"

"Absolutely," said Mummy.

She took a look at the two of them watching her eagerly.

"Absolutely," she said again, smiling. But instead of doing any crossing out, she tore off the whole of the top page and stapled on a brand-new clean one.

This time, in big fat careful letters, she wrote:

Fun for Two
by Jamie

while, safe and happy in Jamie's arms,
Angus took care to watch.

ANNE FINE

The Jamie and Angus Stories

illustrated by
PENNY DALE

Jamie pressed his nose up hard
against the glass and gazed at Angus.
Angus gazed at him. "Oh, please,"
said Jamie. "Please."

From the moment Jamie sets eyes on Angus
in the shop window, he just knows that
they belong together. On Christmas morning
they're finally united, and soon the toy
Highland bull is Jamie's best friend.

ANNE FINE is a distinguished writer for both adults and children. She has won numerous awards for her children's books, including the Carnegie Medal twice, the Whitbread Children's Book of the Year Award twice, the Smarties Book Prize and the Guardian Children's Fiction Prize. In 2001, Anne became Children's Laureate and in 2003, she was awarded an OBE and Fellowship of the Royal Society of Literature. Her other titles for Walker Books include *Care of Henry*; *How to Cross the Road and Not Turn into a Pizza*; *Nag Club*; and the first book in this series, *The Jamie and Angus Stories*. Anne has two grown-up daughters and lives in County Durham.

You can find out more about Anne Fine and her books by visiting her website at **www.annefine.co.uk**

PENNY DALE is one of the UK's leading illustrators of children's books. She has illustrated numerous picture books including *Once There Were Giants*; *Night Night, Cuddly Bear*; and *Rosie's Babies* (shortlisted for the Kate Greenaway Medal and Winner of the Best Books for Babies Award), all written by Martin Waddell; as well as her own stories, *The Boy on the Bus*; *Princess, Princess*; *Ten in the Bed*; *Ten Out of Bed*; *The Elephant Tree*; *Big Brother, Little Brother*; and *Wake Up, Mr B!* (shortlisted for the Kate Greenaway Medal). Penny is married with one daughter and lives in South Wales.

You can find out more about Penny Dale and her books by visiting her website at **www.pennydale.co.uk**